D0623775

AUG 2014

FAERIEGROUND

At the Edge of the Woods

Book Five

BY BETH BRACKEN AND KAY FRASER
ILLUSTRATED BY ODESSA SAWYER

STONE ARCH BOOKS
a capstone imprint

FAERIEGROUND IS PUBLISHED BY
STONE ARCH BOOKS
A CAPSTONE IMPRINT
1710 ROE CREST DRIVE
NORTH MANKATO, MINNESOTA 56003
WWW.CAPSTONEPUB.COM

LIBRARY OF CONGRESS CATALOGING-IN-PUBLICATION
DATA

BRACKEN, BETH.
  AT THE EDGE OF THE WOODS / BY BETH BRACKEN AND
KAY FRASER ; ILLUSTRATED BY ODESSA SAWYER.
    P. CM. -- (FAERIEGROUND ; [BK. 5])
  SUMMARY: ALTHOUGH SOLEDAD AND LUCY ARE
RETURNING TO THE HUMAN WORLD TO SEE THEIR
FAMILIES, THEIR WORK IN THE FAERIEGROUND IS
NOT FINISHED-- WAR THREATENS AND SOLI IS A FAERIE
PRINCESS, SO HER FUTURE LIES THERE.
  ISBN 978-1-4342-4489-5 (LIBRARY BINDING)
1. FAIRIES--JUVENILE FICTION. 2. BEST FRIENDS--
JUVENILE FICTION. 3. IDENTITY (PHILOSOPHICAL
CONCEPT)--JUVENILE FICTION. [1. FAIRIES--FICTION.
2. BEST FRIENDS--FICTION. 3. FRIENDSHIP--FICTION.
4. IDENTITY--FICTION.[1. FRASER, KAY. II. SAWYER,
ODESSA, ILL. III. TITLE. IV. SERIES: BRACKEN, BETH.
FAERIEGROUND ; [BK. 5]

  PZ7.B6989AT 2013
  813.6--DC23

                        2013004211

BOOK DESIGN BY K. FRASER
ALL PHOTOS © SHUTTERSTOCK WITH THESE
EXCEPTIONS: AUTHOR PORTRAIT © K FRASER AND
ILLUSTRATOR PORTRAIT © ODESSA SAWYER

PRINTED IN THE UNITED STATES OF AMERICA
IN STEVENS POINT, WISCONSIN.
032013
007227WZF13

"Hope is the thing with feathers–"

Emily Dickinson

For my parents, Tom and Susan Bracken, who taught me how to build a nest. —b

Dedicado a mi abuela Luisa Zorrilla, el angel que me enseño a volar. —k

Not so long ago, a girl was wished into faerieground . . .

She was alone. She didn't know what to expect on the other side of the faerie curtain. She knew a little bit about the faeries, but only what she'd learned from stories. Only what she'd heard in whispers.

Chapter 1

Soli

I can't stop thinking about my
other mother.

My real mother, my mom, the one who adopted me. I don't know the whole story, of course. There's so much left to learn.

Lucy's mother, Andria, was the one who gave me to her. How did Andria explain me to my mother? How did she convince her? How much does she know?

Does she love me?

She must love me. She and my father both must love me. Did they know I would leave them one day?

Do they know who I am? Did they know who I would become? Did they know all along I was a princess?

Kheelan, who knows these woods so well, is leading Lucy and me to the clearing where the big willow tree stands in the middle of the forest. We are heading home.

The door is in the tree. The path home. The way I came in, the way I'll return.

My wings are heavy on my back.

We are quiet. I can hear the creek nearby, and I know that in the woods, Calandra's armies follow us. Every few steps, a twig snaps, a leaf rustles. Kheelan shoots me a glance, and I nod.

Yes, I heard it. He nods back. We both heard the noise, and we both know what it means. I'm surprised, but not surprised. He and I can talk without saying a word.

We are in real danger, I understand. We aren't being pursued; we're being tracked. And when Lucy and I leave, Kheelan will still be here, and he'll still be in danger.

They are angry. Whoever Calandra's people are, they're angry.

I stripped the queen—my real mother—of her powers. Of course her armies are angry. I should have known they would be.

There is a battle ahead of us, I know that now. But before the battle can begin, I have things to do at home.

So we trudge on, slowly, softly through the woods. Suddenly I notice that Kheelan is holding my hand.

Above us, a crow cries.

Chapter 2

Lucy

Her wings! I can't stop staring at them.

As Soli and Kheelan lead me through the woods, I think about what I've learned in the last few hours.

Soli is a princess. Her mother is a human woman who was a cruel tyrant in the faerie kingdom. We're going home to tell my mother that I need to return to the faerieground and fight. We're going home to tell Soli's parents what we know.

Soli is a princess, a faerie princess.

Also, she's totally holding hands with Kheelan.

When we get to the big old tree in the middle of the woods, we stop.

Soli shifts her body, stretching her arms. Her wings shimmer in the light streaming through the trees.

She smiles when she sees me looking at them. "I'm never going to get used to these," she says.

"Me either," I say, and just like that I can stop worrying about things changing: we are just Soli and Lucy, best friends, again.

Kheelan pushes leaves away from the tree's roots. "Do you know what to do?" he asks.

I'm used to being the leader, the one in charge, the one with the plan, so I say, "No."

But he's not looking at me. Of course he isn't. He's looking at Soli. "I think so," she says.

Soli takes off her crown and hands it to Kheelan. She closes her eyes for a moment, and her wings disappear: not gone, I know, but hidden.

I look at the crown. "Could I——could I hold it?" I ask.

Kheelan passes it to me. It's still warm from resting on Soli's head.

It doesn't look like much, this crown. Almost like a bundle of twigs. It's very old, and somehow feels brittle and strong at the same time.

I think about the fact that it sat on the bottom of a lake for so long, and that makes me shiver.

Kheelan clears his throat, and I look up. "Sorry," I mutter, and hand the crown back to him.

"That's okay," Soli says. "But we do have to go now."

It's so strange, I think, how quickly my friend has become brave.

"It must be strange," Kheelan says, looking at me. For a second I think he's read my mind. Then he says, "To discover that your friend is a princess, and has been all along, without you knowing it."

Soli frowns. "I'm the same," she says. "And since Lucy is more like my sister, it's almost as if we're both royalty."

I laugh, but it feels flat and false.

"I didn't mean——" Kheelan begins, but I stop him.

"I know," I say. "And yes. It is strange."

"I have the feeling it isn't the last strange thing you'll see here," he tells me.

"But first, back home," Soli says. She steps forward and kneels down. She puts a palm on a root and turns to look up at Kheelan.

They stretch their hands to touch. "I'll be back soon," she says.

"I know," he says. "Be safe, but hurry. There's so much to do, and so much still to explain. Come back as soon as you can."

"I will," she says, and then takes my hand, and then we are gone.

Chapter 3

Soli

"Why didn't you tell me?" I ask Andria.

She sits across from me in the living room, her arm around Lucy. They have hugged and cried and now we sit.

I need answers. Andria has them.

She shrugs. "Soli, you can't possibly understand," she says.

That makes me angry. Andria has never treated me like a little kid before. "Oh, really?" I say. "What part couldn't I understand? The part where you pretended to care about me? Or the part where I thought I knew my own life?"

She sighs. "That isn't what I meant," she says, her voice almost a whisper.

Lucy turns to her mother. "Maybe you could just try to explain it to us," she says. Then she glances at me. "Soli has been through a lot. This is hard for her."

Lucy is protecting me again. Just like she always has. At first I feel a warm glow, and I want to thank her. But then I remember who I am. I do not need her protection.

Not anymore.

"Don't, Lucy," I say, and I see hurt fall across my friend's face.

Andria sees it too, and frowns. "I'll tell you what I can," she says, tightening her grip on Lucy's arms. "But you might not like all of it, and I can't tell you everything."

I can see that this will have to be good enough.

She takes a deep breath. "Did you meet the Old Ones?" she asks us. "The Ladybirds?"

Lucy frowns, but I nod. "Yes," I say.

"They're the ones who brought you to me," Andria says. "You were almost two."

I gasp. "I thought I was a baby," I say.

Andria smiles, remembering. "No," she tells me. "You were two. You were talking, and walking. You loved to sing."

She stands up and walks to the window, looking outside. "They came in from the woods and brought you to me, and gave me the Seal, and told me to keep you safe," she says. "I couldn't do it alone; I had Lucy."

Lucy and I look at each other. I know what she's thinking: that we had two years before we became friends. That two years went by in which we didn't know each other.

"That's crazy," Lucy says.

"I know it's not what you believed," Andria tells us. "But it's the truth, and I'm sorry I had to keep it from you, but I did."

"So the faerie offerings," Lucy says. "The things you leave at the edge of the woods. They were to protect Soli?"

"Not exactly," Andria says, a faraway look on her face. "The Seal protected Soli. And mostly, Soli's parents protected her."

"How did they get stuck with me?" I ask. Angry tears are struggling behind my eyes.

Andria smiles, a soft, gentle smile. "They didn't get stuck with you," she explains. "They wished for you."

"I don't understand," I tell her. "How did you know to give me to them?"

She smiles. "They wanted you. They wanted a child so much."

"But how did you know?" I ask.

Andria looks out the window again. The room is quiet. Finally, she says, "I filled a jar with fireflies and let their light guide me. And that is all I can tell you."

Chapter 4

Lucy

"I have to go back, Mom,"
I say, squeezing my mother's
hand.

"I know," she says. "I don't like it, but I know you have to go with Soli."

She packs some things for us: a wicker basket stuffed with peanut butter sandwiches, a thermos of broth, two small cartons of berries.

Soli hugs her, and then waits outside.

My mom wraps her arms around me and squeezes tight. "Please be careful," she says. "I couldn't tell you everything, but you need to know that you can't trust everyone there."

"I know," I say. "I think Queen Calandra won't be dangerous anymore, but—"

She pulls away. "Calandra was never dangerous," she says.

"She wasn't?" I ask, confused.

Mom shakes her head. "She had dangerous powers," she says. "She controlled too many people, and some of them are dangerous. But she—"

She wants to say more, I can tell. But doesn't.

And I don't have time to ask.

I lift the basket and kiss my mom's cheek one last time. Then I leave, closing the door gently behind me.

"Ready?" I ask Soli.

"I think so," she says.

But before we've reached the end of the path to the street, my mom runs out. "Wait!" she says. "Lucy, please come back. Just for a minute."

I go back, and she closes the door, keeping Soli outside. "What's up?" I ask. My mom's eyes are wild.

"Come home the second anything starts to feel wrong," she says.

"The whole thing feels wrong, Mom," I say. "I mean, it's scary, and I don't know anyone, and at least Soli is, like, *from* there."

"I'm—" she begins.

"I'll be safe," I say. "Don't worry."

A tear slides down my mom's face. "Just promise," she says. "Come home if you notice—if anything goes wrong."

"I promise," I say.

"Okay," Mom says. She takes a deep breath. "I guess that's all I can ask for."

And then I leave, quickly, before I can change my mind.

Chapter 5

Soli

"I knew you were never mine to keep,"
my mother says.

"Yes, I was," I say. "I still am."

We stand in the doorway. Lucy is waiting
at the bottom of the sidewalk. I don't really
know what to say. My mom isn't my real
mother, but she's still my mom. And now she
knows who I really am.

"Do you know what you'll have to do . . .
there?" she asks.

I shrug. "Not really," I say. "I'm still figuring it
out. I don't really know who I am supposed to
be there."

She sighs. "I know you're still my daughter," she says. "I'll always know that."

"I know, Mom," I say.

"I hope so," she says.

"Andria said you wished for me," I tell her. "Did you?"

She smiles. "For my whole life," she says. She hugs me—a quick, tight embrace. "Now go, and be safe," she says. "And if—"

A tear falls from her eye.

"If you can come back," she says, "this will always be your home."

Chapter 6

Lucy

Kheelan waits for us at the edge of the woods.

"What are you doing here?" Soli asks. "I thought you couldn't cross over."

"It's important," he says. He looks up at the sky, and then back at Soli. "I had to make sure you were returning. Something has happened."

"Why wouldn't we return?" I ask, confused.

He takes Soli's hand and we hurry through the forest. I try to keep up with them. Kheelan calls back over his shoulder, "I thought someone would try to keep her here."

Of course. It wouldn't matter if I didn't return.

"What happened?" Soli asks Kheelan.

"The Crows have sent a messenger," he says. "They want Calandra back. Before she can tell us anything."

"Who are the Crows?" I ask, but no one listens to me.

"Why would she tell us anything?" Soli asks.

Kheelan shakes his head. "Because she still wants you," he says.

Soli doesn't say much after that. And soon we are at the willow tree that marks the entrance to the faerieground.

"Do I have to make a wish again?" Soli asks. "How do we get back?"

Kheelan smiles. "No, of course not. It's your land to enter, now. It will be different for the human, but if we both take her hand, she'll be allowed through."

The human? "I have a name," I mutter.

Soli doesn't hear me. "I thought it was sort
of always my land to enter," she says, running
a hand along the side of the tree's trunk. "I
mean, if I've been the princess all along."

"Yes, it was," Kheelan says. "I don't know the
whole story. I think the Ladybirds kept you
protected, somehow, until you needed to
rescue Lucy. Then your need was greater. In
a way, that's how Calandra ended up tricking
you into coming back to the kingdom."

"Don't we need to hurry?" I say.

Kheelan glances me. "Oh, yes. Of course. Let's go."

They take my hands and we leave our woods and find ourselves back in faerieground.

Chapter 7

Soli

The Crows live in the darkest part of the forest.

It's almost as if I don't need to be told who these people are, but Kheelan tells me anyway as we find our way to the castle.

The Crows. They're the ones who sent my mother—Calandra—to the kingdom.

She had one task: make the king fall in love with her.

Or maybe two tasks, I suppose. The second was to kill him.

"I don't understand why," I say.

We are within sight of the palace now. Kheelan shrugs. "To take control, I suppose. The ruler of our kingdom harnesses strong magic. I don't know much about everything Calandra has controlled. I just know it's a lot." He smiles at me and adds, "And now you control it."

Then he pulls my crown out of his satchel. "I almost forgot," he says, and places it on my head. I feel the burn of the wings rippling from my back.

A princess, again.

But then I hear Lucy moan.

"What's wrong?" I ask, turning. I've been too busy listening to Kheelan. I haven't checked to see if we were walking too fast for Lucy, or if she was tired or hungry. We have just been hurrying through the forest, staying quiet.

"I just have a headache," she says, wiping a little tear from her eye. "I'm sorry."

Kheelan seems to ignore her. "We can't stop now," he says. "The messenger is in the prison. They're waiting for you to talk to him."

"The same prison I was in?" Lucy asks.

I shudder, thinking of my best friend trapped in a dungeon cell. "We have to find somewhere else for prisoners to stay," I say. "If we have to have prisoners."

Kheelan shoots me a glance. "Of course we have to have prisoners," he says. "We're fighting a war, aren't we?"

"My head hurts so much," Lucy whispers.

A war?

Chapter 8

Lucy

My head is throbbing. It's all I can think about.

"I need to lie down," I say. My words sound far away.

"I guess I didn't know this was a war," Soli says.

"What did you think it was?" asks Kheelan. "Why did you think the palace was falling apart?" We are walking through the gates, and he gestures to the giant stone building.

Some of the stones are cracked. Many of the windows have broken or missing glass. And I know that inside, cobwebs and dirt float in the air.

"I don't know," Soli says quietly. "I thought she was just a bad queen."

Finally, we are inside the castle. Again, louder, I say, "Please, you guys, I really need to lie down."

"Oh, Lucy!" Soli says, rushing to my side. "Your face is so white!"

Kheelan finally looks at me. "She looks awful," he says. "When did your headache start?"

"Right when we got to the faerieground," I say.

"The sickness," Kheelan mutters.

Soli brushes my hair out of my eyes. "What's the sickness?" she asks.

He shrugs. "I've never seen it before," he says. "But then again, Lucy is the first human I've met here."

"So it only affects humans?" Soli asks.

My head feels like there's a drum pounding inside. "What about . . . the queen?" I ask slowly.

"She was under a spell," Kheelan says. "The stories say that the sickness protects us from humans." He looks down the hall. "Come on. Let's find her somewhere to rest."

"Why didn't it happen before?" I ask. "I was here for days."

"Because of the spell, I guess," says Kheelan. "A faerie wished you here." He looks at Soli and smiles. "A half-faerie, anyway."

They lead me down the corridor toward the rooms where Calandra lived.

Inside her room, the air still smells like her. My head hurts so badly that the candlelight is too bright to look at.

"Will this go away?" I ask, lying down on the sofa, covering my eyes. "Is there a cure?"

Then, from the bedroom, we hear a low moan.

"That's my mother," Soli whispers.

Chapter 9

Soli

A girl rushes out of the queen's bedroom.

"Who are you?" I ask.

But Lucy is smiling. "Caro?" she says happily. "What are you doing here?" She looks at me and explains, "We were in the cell together."

"As soon as you left, they put Calandra in with me," the girl says. She sits down next to Lucy, and I have to make room. "And right away, I could tell she had the sickness. She couldn't even open her eyes."

"So you brought her here?" Kheelan asks. "How? Why?"

Caro shrugs. "The princess was gone," she says, smoothing Lucy's hair. "The queen wasn't the queen anymore. And she was sick. Only under Queen Calandra would someone sick have spent the night in a cell." She looks directly at me and adds, "I was under the impression that things had changed."

"You did the right thing," I say. "She's in there?"

"Yes," Caro says. "But I don't think she'll last much longer. She needs the Ladybirds." She looks back to Lucy and adds, "And by the looks of it, so does she."

Kheelan frowns. "We don't have time to go all the way to the Ladybirds," he says. "The messenger from the Crows is here. Remember? They need an answer."

Everyone stares at me. I square my shoulders and stand up.

"Then," I say, "I guess I'll go and talk to him." I look at Kheelan. "You'll have to take them to the Ladybirds. Can you do it?"

He sighs. But then he nods.

I leave and walk down the hall toward the prison cells.

I'm afraid. I should have asked Kheelan to wait, to come with me.

But he needs to take Calandra—my mother— and Lucy to the Ladybirds. I can't let anything happen to Lucy. And I don't want my mother to die, either, even though she seems awful.

Even if she's awful, she loves me, somehow.

My sneakers scuff along the stone floor.

Then I hear a sound. Footsteps hurrying toward me.

"Wait," says a man's voice.

My heart turns cold.

I'm afraid to wait, but I know I can't outrun anyone. Especially these people, with all their unknown powers. So I stop, and I turn.

It's one of the guards. "Wait, princess," he says, rushing down the hall.

He reaches me, out of breath. "Are you going to speak with the Crow?" he asks.

"It is none of your business where I'm going," I say, trying to make myself as tall as possible, trying to speak clearly without letting my voice shake, trying not to let him see how frightened I am.

"You can't go alone," he says. "I'll come with you. I am Jonn."

"No," I say. "You must leave this palace."

The guard—Jonn—frowns. "You don't understand, princess," he says. "That messenger is dangerous. The Crows are dangerous, far worse than you can imagine. You need protection."

"Calandra isn't the queen anymore," I say. "That means you don't work here anymore, either."

I turn to leave, but he grabs my arm. His touch is gentle.

The guard smiles.

"You don't understand," he says. "I work for the queen. I worked for the last queen, and the one before that. I don't work for Calandra. I work for the queen." He bows deeply and adds, "And now I work for you."

Chapter 10

Lucy

We go to the Ladybirds by the edge of the woods.

I can hardly see, but Kheelan leads me, and Caro leads Calandra. It's amazing how quickly she has aged. She used to seem like a timeless queen. Now she seems like a middle-aged lady. One who's in a lot of pain.

I remember one summer when my mother was sick. She spent the whole summer inside. I was only five or six.

That entire summer, the house was shut. It was a dusty, dark summer. I tried to play outside when I could. I stayed at Soli's whenever I could.

I remember how she looked that summer, my mother.

She looked dried-out and limp. Her lips were cracked. Her hair was straw. She wasn't my mother.

That's what Calandra looks like. And that's how I feel.

The walk through the woods is torture. Every step makes my head throb.

"Why is this happening?" Calandra moans.

Kheelan laughs, a short, mean laugh. "You deserve worse," he says.

"That's not fair," Caro mutters.

Kheelan stops and releases my arm. "Why not?" he says angrily. "She killed our king. She sent the kingdom into ruin. Hundreds of us have died. Our people have starved."

Calandra stands up as straight as her pain will let her. "I loved him," she says. "No one ever believed me, but I loved him. And he knew."

Chapter 11

Soli

When I see the man in the cell, I'm glad I have a guard.

"Keep away from her," Jonn warns after he throws open the heavy door.

The man is huge, like a tree. His hair is a shock of black. His eyes are black, too.

If the rest of his people look like him, I can see why they are called the Crows.

"So, this is the little princess?" the man says slowly, looking me up and down.

I draw myself up as tall as I can. "I am Soli."

"Mikael," the man says. "Of the Crows. I heard that you broke Calandra's spell, so I've come to bring you to our people. Or else the battle begins."

I look at Jonn. His face is still.

"I won't go with you," I say.

The man—Mikael—laughs. "Then we are at war," he says. "And I hope you're ready to become the leader of a failed army."

"I thought we were already at war," I mutter.

Mikael shrugs. "In a way," he says. "But I suppose you don't know anything about it. Isn't that true?"

"I know enough," I say, but he just laughs.

There is a tiny window set up high in the wall. Through it, I hear someone running toward the palace. Jonn is instantly alert. He stands straight, listening.

"That won't be my people attacking, if you're concerned," Mikael says. "We are fast, but not that fast."

Then he looks at me. "But it will be soon," he says. "And you won't be ready."

"You know nothing about me," I say.

He laughs again. "I know your name," he tells me. "I know your age. I know your mother, and I knew your grandmother. I know how you came here. I know where you live."

Outside, the footsteps are louder. "And," Mikael says calmly, "I know you've sent your friends to the Ladybirds. And princess? I know how to find them."

Beth & Kay

Kay Fraser and *Beth Bracken* are a designer-editor team in Minnesota.

Kay is from Buenos Aires. She left home at eighteen and moved to North Dakota—basically the exact opposite of Argentina. These days, she designs books, writes, makes tea for her husband, and drives her daughters to their dance lessons.

Beth and her husband live in a light-filled house with their son, Sam. She spends her time editing, reading, daydreaming, and rearranging her furniture.

Kay and Beth both love dark chocolate, Buffy, and tea.

Odessa

Odessa Sawyer is an illustrator from Santa Fe, New Mexico. She works mainly in digital mixed media, utilizing digital painting, photography, and traditional pen and ink.

Odessa's work has graced the book covers of many top publishing houses, and she has also done work for various film and television projects, posters, and album covers.

Highly influenced by fantasy, fairy tales, fashion, and classic horror, Odessa's work celebrates a whimsical, dreamy and vibrant quality.